Monster Mayhem

Early★Reader

First American edition published in 2022 by Lerner Publishing Group, Inc.

An original concept by Katie Dale
Copyright © 2022 Katie Dale

Illustrated by Dean Gray

First published by Maverick Arts Publishing Limited

Maverick
arts publishing

Licensed Edition
Monster Mayhem

Lerner Publications Company
An imprint of Lerner Publishing Group, Inc.
241 First Avenue North
Minneapolis, MN 55401 USA

For reading levels and more information, look up this title at www.lernerbooks.com.

Main body text set in Mikado. Typeface provided by HVD Fonts.

Library of Congress Cataloging-in-Publication Data

Names: Dale, Katie, author. | Gray, Dean, illustrator.
Title: Monster mayhem / Katie Dale ; illustrated by Dean Gray.
Description: First American edition. | Minneapolis : Lerner Publications, 2022.
  | Series: Early bird readers. Blue (Early bird stories) | "First published by
  Maverick Arts Publishing Limited"—Page facing title page. | Audience:
  Ages 4–8. | Audience: Grades K–1. | Summary: "Little monsters don't have
  time for sleep. They must prove they're the scariest of them all! With
  illustrations and a reading comprehension quiz"—Provided by publisher.
Identifiers: LCCN 2021043259 (print) | LCCN 2021043260 (ebook)
  | ISBN 9781728438443 (lib. bdg.) | ISBN 9781728448329 (pbk.) |
  ISBN 9781728444536 (eb pdf)
Subjects: LCSH: Readers (Primary) | LCGFT: Readers (Publications)
Classification: LCC PE1119.2 .D3525 2022 (print) | LCC PE1119.2 (ebook) |
  DDC 428.6/2—dc23

LC record available at https://lccn.loc.gov/2021043259
LC ebook record available at https://lccn.loc.gov/2021043260

Manufactured in the United States of America
1-49667-49587-9/8/2021

Monster Mayhem

Katie Dale
illustrated by Dean Gray

Lerner Publications ◆ Minneapolis

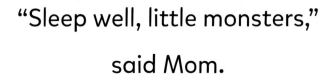

"Sleep well, little monsters," said Mom.

"Do not let the bedbugs bite!"
said Dad.

"I cannot sleep," said little Sniff.

"What if the bedbugs bite me?"

"I will frighten them off!" said Wiff.

"For I am the most scary monster of all."

"I will frighten off the bedbugs
with my horrid monster SMELL!"

"You do stink," said Tiff.

"But I am the most scary monster of all."

"For I will frighten off the bedbugs with my sharp monster NAILS!"

"You do have the sharpest nails,"

said Biff.

"But I am the most scary monster
of all."

"For I will frighten off the bedbugs
with my big monster TEETH!"

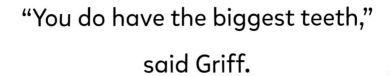

"You do have the biggest teeth,"
said Griff.

"But I am the most scary monster of all."

"For I have the biggest roar!"

"I will frighten off the bedbugs
with my big monster . . ."

The little monsters ran back into bed.

"Mom will frighten off the bedbugs," said Biff.

"She is the most scary monster!" said Wiff.

They all agreed.

Quiz

1. Why can't Sniff sleep?
   a) Bedbugs might bite him
   b) Monsters might scare him
   c) It's too dark

2. How would Wiff scare the bedbugs?
   a) With his hair
   b) With his horns
   c) With his smell

3. How would Biff scare the bedbugs?
   a) With his hands
   b) With his teeth
   c) With his eyes

4. What does the monsters' mom shout?
    a) BOO!
    b) WAA!
    c) ROAR!

5. Who is the most scary monster?
    a) Sniff
    b) Mom
    c) Griff

Leveled for Guided Reading

Early Bird Stories have been edited and leveled by leading educational consultants to correspond with guided reading levels. The levels are assigned by taking into account the content, language style, layout, and phonics used in each book. Visit www.lernerbooks.com for more Early Bird Readers titles!

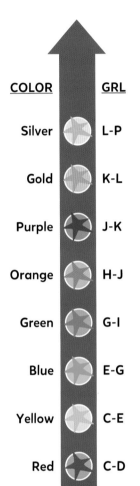

COLOR	GRL
Silver	L-P
Gold	K-L
Purple	J-K
Orange	H-J
Green	G-I
Blue	E-G
Yellow	C-E
Red	C-D
Pink	A-C